What Kids Say About
Carole Marsh Mysteries . . .

"I love the real locations! Reading the book always makes me want to go and visit them all on our next family vacation. My Mom says maybe, but I can't wait!"

"One day, I want to be a real kid in one of Ms. Marsh's mystery books. I think it would be fun, and I think I am a real character anyway. I filled out the application and sent it in and am keeping my fingers crossed!"

"History was not my favorite subject till I starting reading Carole Marsh Mysteries. Ms. Marsh really brings history to life. Also, she leaves room for the scary and fun."

"I think Christina is so smart and brave. She is lucky to be in the mystery books because she gets to go to a lot of places. I always wonder just how much of the book is true and what is made up. Trying to figure that out is fun!"

"Grant is cool and funny! He makes me laugh a lot!!"

"I like that there are boys and girls in the story of different ages. Some mysteries I outgrow, but I can always find a favorite character to identify with in these books."

"They are scary, but not too scary. They are funny. I learn a lot. There is always food which makes me hungry. I feel like I am there."

What Parents and Teachers Say About Carole Marsh Mysteries . . .

"I think kids love these books because they have such a wealth of detail. I know I learn a lot reading them! It's an engaging way to look at the history of any place or event. I always say I'm only going to read one chapter to the kids, but that never happens—it's always two or three, at least!"
—Librarian

"Reading the mystery and going on the field trip—Scavenger Hunt in hand—was the most fun our class ever had! It really brought the place and its history to life. They loved the real kids characters and all the humor. I loved seeing them learn that reading is an experience to enjoy!"
—4th grade teacher

"Carole Marsh is really on to something with these unique mysteries. They are so clever; kids want to read them all. The Teacher's Guides are chock full of activities, recipes, and additional fascinating information. My kids thought I was an expert on the subject—and with this tool, I felt like it!"
—3rd grade teacher

"My students loved writing their own Real Kids/Real Places mystery book! Ms. Marsh's reproducible guidelines are a real jewel. They learned about copyright and more & ended up with their own book they were so proud of!"
—Reading/Writing Teacher

"The kids seem very realistic—my children seemed to relate to the characters. Also, it is educational by expanding their knowledge about the famous places in the books."

"They are what children like: mysteries and adventures with children they can relate to."

"Encourages reading for pleasure."

"This series is great. It can be used for reluctant readers, and as a history supplement."

The Mystery of the

Ancient
Pyramid
Cairo, Egypt

by Carole Marsh

Copyright ©2006 Carole Marsh/ Gallopade International
Manufactured in Peachtree City, GA
Ebook edition Copyright ©2011
All rights reserved.

Carole Marsh Mysteries™ and its skull colophon are the property of Carole Marsh and Gallopade International.

Published by Gallopade International/Carole Marsh Books. Printed in the United States of America.

Managing Editor: Sherry Moss
Cover Design: Michele Winkelman
Some photos courtesy of Steve Winkelman
King Tut Riddles courtesy of Michael Longmeyer

Picture Credits:
The publisher would like to thank the following for their kind permission to reproduce the cover photographs.

Alex Kitching, Hartlepool, United Kingdom *Hieroglyphs*;
©2006 Stephen O'Dell *Khafre's Pyramid, The Great Sphinx of Giza*;
© Scott Rothstein | Agency: Dreamstime.com *Mummy*; **Kaspars Upmanis, Ogre, Ogres raj., Latvia** *Smiling Camel*

Gallopade International is introducing SAT words that kids need to know in each new book we publish. The SAT words are bold in the story. Look for this special logo beside each word in the glossary. Happy Learning!

Gallopade is proud to be a member and supporter of these educational organizations and associations:

American Booksellers Association
American Library Association
International Reading Association
National Association for Gifted Children
The National School Supply and Equipment Association
The National Council for the Social Studies
Museum Store Association
Association of Partners for Public Lands
Association of Booksellers for Children
Association for the Study of African American Life and History
National Alliance of Black School Educators

30 Years Ago . . .

As a mother and an author, one of the fondest periods of my life was when I decided to write mystery books for children. At this time (1979) kids were pretty much glued to the TV, something parents and teachers complained about the way they do about web surfing and blogging today.

I decided to set each mystery in a real place—a place kids could go and visit for themselves after reading the book. And I also used real children as characters. Usually a couple of my own children served as characters, and I had no trouble recruiting kids from the book's location to also be characters.

Also, I wanted all the kids—boys and girls of all ages—to participate in solving the mystery. And, I wanted kids to learn something as they read. Something about the history of the location. And I wanted the stories to be funny. That formula of real+scary+smart+fun served me well.

I love getting letters from teachers and parents who say they read the book with their class or child, then visited the historic site and saw all the places in the mystery for themselves. What's so great about that? What's great is that you and your children have an experience that bonds you together forever. Something you shared. Something you both cared about at the time. Something that crossed all age levels—a good story, a good scare, a good laugh!

30 years later,

Carole Marsh

Hey, kids! As you see—here we are ready to embark on another of our exciting Carole Marsh Mystery adventures! You know, in "real life," I keep very close tabs on Christina, Grant, and their friends when we travel. However, in the mystery books, they always seem to slip away from Papa and me so that they can try to solve the mystery on their own!

I hope you will go to www.carolemarshmysteries.com and apply to be a character in a future mystery book! Well, the *Mystery Girl* is all tuned up and ready for "take-off!"

Gotta go...Papa says so! Wonder what I've forgotten this time?

Happy "Armchair Travel" Reading,

Mimi

About the Characters

 **Christina**, age 10: Mysterious things really do happen to her! Hobbies: soccer, Girl Scouts, anything crafty, hanging out with Mimi, and going on new adventures.

 **Grant**, age 7: Always manages to fall off boats, back into cactuses, and find strange clues—even in real life! Hobbies: camping, baseball, computer games, math, and hanging out with Papa.

 **Mimi** is Carole Marsh, children's book author and creator of Carole Marsh Mysteries, Around the World in 80 Mysteries, Three Amigos Mysteries, Criss, Cross, Applesauce Detective Agency Mysteries, and many others.

 **Papa** is Bob Longmeyer, the author's real-life husband, who really does wear a tuxedo, cowboy boots and hat, fly an airplane, captain a boat, speak in a booming voice, and laugh a lot!

Travel around the world with Christina and Grant as they visit famous places in 80 countries, and experience the mysterious happenings that always seem to follow them!

Around the World in 80 Mysteries

Books in This Series

#1 The Mystery at Big Ben
(London, England)

#2 The Mystery at the Eiffel Tower
(Paris, France)

#3 The Mystery at the Roman Colosseum
(Rome, Italy)

#4 The Mystery of the Ancient Pyramid
(Cairo, Egypt)

#5 The Mystery on the Great Wall of China
(Beijing, China)

#6 The Mystery on the Great Barrier Reef
(Australia)

#7 The Mystery at Mt. Fuji
(Tokyo, Japan)

#8 The Mystery in the Amazon Rainforest
(South America)

#9 The Mystery at Dracula's Castle
(Transylvania, Romania)

#10 The Curse of the Acropolis
(Athens, Greece)

#11 The Mystery at the Crystal Castle
(Bavaria, Germany)

#12 The Mystery in Icy Antarctica

#13 The Rip-Roaring Mystery on the African Safari
(South Africa)

#14 The Breathtaking Mystery on Mount Everest
(The Top of the World)

Table of Contents

1 "Tut, tut!" 1
2 Pharaoh in Cairo 5
3 Sphinx, Sphinx, You Stink! 11
4 Welcome to Civilization? 17
5 Walk Like An Egyptian 21
6 Piles of Pyramids. 27
7 No Clue? 35
8 Gold! 41
9 A Curse? Of Course!. 49
10 Eenie, Meenie, Mummy, Mo. 55
11 Nile, Nile, Crocodile 63
12 Unlucky Luxor. 69
13 The Amazing Karnak. 75
14 Belly Dancing. 81
15 Valley of the Kings. 87
16 Water Over the Dam 95
17 The Spitting Camel 101
18 Are You My Mummy? 105
19 Oh, Rats! 107
20 A Date in the Oasis 111
   Glossary. 118
   Built-In Book Club. 120
   Hieroglyph Alphabet 124
   Egyptian Fast Facts 126
   About the Author. 131
   Write Your Own Mystery. 132

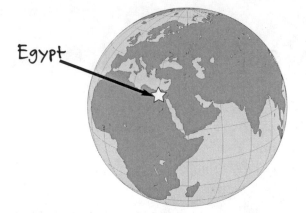

Egypt

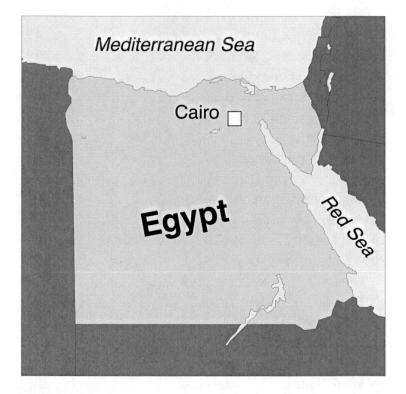

Mediterranean Sea

Cairo

Egypt

Red Sea

"Tut, tut!"

"All I know about the country of Egypt is King Tut," said Christina. "But I can't wait to learn and see more—much more!"

Christina, age 10, was more excited than she had been in a long time. She often traveled around the world with her grandmother, famous children's mystery book author Carole Marsh...her grandfather Papa, the pilot cowboy...and, of course, her brother Grant, age 7. But they had never before been any place as exotic and mysterious as the country of Egypt.

"Hey, Mimi," called Grant in a loud voice. He was sitting with his sister in the back of the small red and white airplane, *The Mystery Girl*. "Are you going to write a mystery book on this trip?"

Grant and Christina both leaned as far

forward as their seatbelts would allow to hear their grandmother's answer.

Mimi laughed. "Well, Grant, you know how I usually say NO MYSTERY when we travel...so I can just relax and have a good time? This time, it's a no-brainer—how can I come to ancient Egypt, land of pyramids, pharaohs, and many, many mummies—and NOT write a mystery? Of course I'm going to write a mystery!"

Grant and Christina giggled and gave a "thumbs up" gesture. Their grandfather, Papa, roared with laughter above the noisy propeller of the plane he was piloting.

"An honest woman!" he proclaimed. "You usually tease us that there won't be a mystery, but we know better, don't we kids?"

Mimi blushed and laughed and tossed her blond hair in the wind. "And you kids always promise you won't get involved and try to help me solve any mystery," their grandmother reminded them. "And then you always do...and end up getting into big trouble!"

"But BIG TROUBLE is half the fun," argued Grant.

"And how would you ever solve a real mystery without us, anyway?" asked Christina. "You have to admit that we are a big help."

"NOT!" cried Mimi. "I always have to worry about you and hunt for you and explain why you have been places and done things that you just aren't supposed to do," she insisted.

"But who cares as long as the mystery gets solved?" asked Christina.

"Yeah," added Grant, "who cares?"

At the top of their lungs both Mimi and Papa screamed back from the cockpit: "YOUR PARENTS DO, THAT'S WHO!"

Christina and Grant laughed. They both thought that this was the trip of a lifetime and would be great fun. Of course, it was a little warm in the airplane. And the shimmering desert undulating below them looked like a terrible place to have to make any emergency landing. And mummies were pretty creepy. And they could certainly do without any of those ancient curses that they had heard about.

So, how could these two innocent children have known that they would soon encounter curses, mummies, lots of heat, a "crash landing" of sorts, and a mystery that they never imagined, and, as Christina would say before it was all over: "We could have done without!"

Pharaoh in Cairo

Soon, Papa was winging the plane down to a smooth landing on a small airfield with runways covered in a glistening coat of sand. It was like landing on a sugar cookie, Christina thought.

As they taxied down the runway to the terminal, Christina felt cold goosebumps tickle up and down her spine. Then she felt a little letdown. "All airports look alike," she grumbled to herself.

"Not this one," argued Grant. "See that guy? He's wearing his pajamas—right out here in public!"

"Those aren't his nightclothes," Mimi explained. "He's wearing the traditional clothing many men here wear."

Grant and Christina stared at the long, white

cotton dress (or at least that's what they thought it looked like), twisted turban on his head, and the scarf around his neck, and giggled.

"Papa, you would look handsome in an outfit like that," Christina teased her grandfather.

"I am certain I would," Papa insisted seriously and Mimi nodded in agreement.

"Papa wore a skirt once," Grant reminded them.

"It was a kilt," Papa corrected.

As they neared the terminal, Grant said, "Look at that funny writing." He motioned to various signs posted on the wall of the terminal. "Those are **hieroglyphs**, right?"

"Not quite," said Mimi. "That writing is in Arabic. You'll know **hieroglyphs** when you see them—trust me."

"Hey, there's a camel!" Christina squealed.

"Maybe he's coming to get our baggage," said Papa.

"Can we ride a camel to town?" Grant asked eagerly.

"No, we cannot!" Mimi insisted. But as usual, their grandmother was full of information to share. "The camel has been used in Egypt for thousands of years as transportation. Their meat, milk, and wool are also used. Plus, they're designed for the heat and sand of the desert. They even have a transparent extra eyelid they use sort of like sunglasses to keep the sand out. And if you watch, you'll see that they walk with two legs on one side, then two legs on the other, sort of rolling along. That's how they got their nickname Ships of the Desert." Mimi rubbed her brow with her lacy handkerchief. "I'm not sure I'm ready for this heat."

"At least you don't have a hump," said Grant.

"Gee, thanks for noticing, Grant," Mimi said.

Papa pulled the airplane into the parking area and let the stairs down. As the kids grabbed their backpacks and hopped out, they stopped cold—or really, they stopped HOT!

"Wow! It really is hot," said Christina.

"And windy," said Grant, gritting some sand between his teeth. "Sand-wiches," he grumbled to himself.

Suddenly, a very handsome tanned man with glistening white hair dressed in a suit, white shirt, and tie strode forward across the tarmac to greet them. He looked cool, relaxed, and charming.

"Welcome!" he said as he approached *The*

Mystery Girl.

"I am here to officially welcome your family to Egypt," he cried in a deep, jovial voice. "And to aid Mimi with her mystery!"

Papa helped Mimi down the steps of the plane. "Zahi Hawass!" she said in delight, extending her hand which the man took and kissed. Mimi smiled. "It is so kind of you to meet us."

"What's up?" Grant whispered to his sister. "Mimi usually says 'no mystery.'"

"Grant, she always says that," said Christina. "She doesn't really mean it, anymore than she means that the man shouldn't have come—she's obviously absolutely thrilled that he came to welcome us."

"I don't understand," Grant grumbled.

Christina lowered her eyebrows and gave her brother her "detective" look. "All things will be made clear," she said.

"Don't be so mysterious," Grant said.

Christina smiled. "Why not?" she asked. "It's my job!"

When Grant caught up with Mimi, he asked, "Is that man some kind of funky pharaoh?"

Mimi laughed. "No," she whispered to

Grant. "He's much more famous than that! He's the Secretary General of Egypt's Supreme Council of Antiquities."

"What does that mean?" Grant asked Christina.

"I think it means he's in charge of the mummies!" Christina answered.

"Then he's my new best friend!" said Grant as he skipped across the sandy tarmac into the cool, air-conditioned terminal.

Sphinx, Sphinx, You Stink!

Christina was very frustrated. It seemed like it took forever to get *The Mystery Girl* squared away. Papa was very particular about his airplane. Mimi and Mr. Hawass were sipping cups of *abwa* in the coffee shop. Grant had disappeared to explore something somewhere, as usual. So Christina busied herself by wandering into the gift shop.

She loved to collect business cards and inexpensive souvenirs. The business cards were free, and she liked to pay for her own souvenirs herself with spending money she had earned. Of course, Papa had not yet gone to the money exchange and converted their U.S. dollars into

Egyptian currency, so she just window-shopped.

Christina was admiring the little toy pyramids, leather camels, packs of papyrus paper, and backgammon boards when she spotted something that seemed most peculiar to her.

Outside the shop, a young man in jeans, tennis shoes, a King Tut tee shirt, and a baseball cap snooped around a luggage cart. Perhaps he was looking around for something that belonged to him, but Christina doubted it. The reason she thought so was that he would snoop a little, then stoop a little when someone came by, then stop and look all around as if to make sure no one was watching him.

Suddenly, he grabbed a very handsome leather briefcase from the bottom of the pile of luggage. He tugged hard until it came free, then turned to run. Just then he looked up and saw Christina looking at him. He gave her a mean stare and bumped into her, almost knocking her backpack off her shoulders.

As he started off, Mr. Hawass came running out of the coffee shop and shook his fist and hollered at the man, "Stop, thief! That is my case!!"

Christina continued to stare out the window of the shop in surprise as Mimi joined Mr. Hawass. He threw his hands up in exasperation. "You see what I mean?" he cried. "This is very bad. The plans for the pyramid renovation were in that case!"

Policeman scurried through the airport chasing the man. Christina ran out of the shop just in time to see the young man and the policemen running out of the airport. Mr. Hawass followed them. She heard a big THUD, then saw Grant come limping into the terminal.

"Hey!" he called to his sister. "Some guy just hit me in the knee with a big, brown briefcase. It hurt!"

"Come here," said Mimi. "Where have you been?"

Grant nodded toward the outdoors and rubbed his leg. "Just helping Papa," he said. "He's right behind me."

They all turned and did not see Papa, but Christina thought to ask her brother, "Did the man who hit you with the case see you?"

Grant looked at his sister, puzzled. "I guess so," he said. "I looked at him, so I'm sure he saw me. Why do you ask?"

Mimi was busy looking around for Papa, so Christina bent down and whispered to her brother. "Because that guy just stole something important...and now he knows that you and I can identify him."

"Well, I don't care," said Grant. "When I see him again, I'm going to say 'Sphinx, sphinx, you stink!'...and that will be my curse on him, cause, you know, it reaalllly hurts!"

Mimi dashed back to Grant and stooped down to check his leg. "Are you ok?" she asked. "Is anything broken?" She rubbed Grant's leg so hard that it made him giggle.

"No, no, I promise!" he said. "I think the corner of the case just hit the middle part of my knee; you know, the funny-feeling part. It's feeling better." He wrenched away from his grandmother and stood up. "See...I can walk."

Grant hobbled out of his grandmother's reach as Papa dashed into the terminal. "What's going on?" he asked them. "There's a lot of activity out on the tarmac and a lot of running around."

Mimi explained to Papa what had happened.

"Oh," said Papa nonchalantly after her explanation. "Luggage gets stolen off airport carts all the time I'm sure. That's too bad, but I thought someone had gotten murdered or something."

"Don't say *murdered*," said Mimi in a funny voice.

"Why?" asked Papa, surprised.

"Yeah, Mimi, we know what that word means," Christina said. "Why can't Papa say it?"

Mimi frowned. "I'll tell you later," she said to Papa with a wink that meant "so hush up!"

But Papa and Christina were having none of that! "What murder?" they demanded together.

Mimi shook her blond curls back and forth in exasperation. "You don't understand. There hasn't been a murder...yet."

"Well, what does that mean?" said Papa. "We just landed. How can a mystery involving us be starting so soon?"

"It doesn't involve us," Mimi insisted. "There have just been some threats, and now some important plans have been stolen, and, oh, well, I don't know the whole story, so I don't think we should worry about it."

Papa looked at Christina. "Did you see the man who stole the case?"

Christina nodded.

Now Papa looked at Grant, puzzled. "What's

wrong with your leg? Did you see the man who stole the case?"

When Grant admitted that he had, then Papa said to all of them in a deep and serious and aggravated tone of voice that boomed through the terminal: "THEN I THINK WE SHOULD WORRY!"

Welcome to Civilization?

As they headed into town in a hired car, Christina looked over her map of Egypt. She had always wanted to visit the continent of Africa and go on a safari and see wild animals like lions, tigers, and elephants. So she still felt surprised to be in Egypt instead.

It was fascinating to her to see the desert all around, and yet here on the map surrounding the capital city of Cairo were two seas—the Mediterranean Sea to the north and the Red Sea to the east and south.

Desert and water. Old and new. Alike and different. She thought travel was especially interesting because of all the things you learned that you did not know...and all the things you learned that you were surprised you already knew.

For example, she was surprised to read that more than 90 percent of Egypt was desert. That seemed like a lot of desert! But she was not surprised to learn that most of the 70 million Egyptians lived along the Nile River. She knew that water attracted people for many reasons—to grow crops, to farm animals, to have water for drinking, and to enjoy for recreation and beauty.

Nonetheless, she was astounded to look at her map and see that the famous pyramids were not far out in the desert, but just outside the city. And very quickly, she and Grant were both amazed to learn that Egyptians didn't know how to drive!

"Papa!" Grant squealed. "Look at all this traffic! And they don't seem to be following your 'Rules of the Road.'"

"That's an understatement, Grant," Mimi said, holding tightly to the car door handle. "It's almost dark and no one has their lights on."

"And no one is staying in their lanes," noted Christina. "Or using their turn signals."

Indeed, the city traffic was a nightmare circus

and Grant and Christina didn't know whether to be afraid or to think the whirlwind of crazy drivers was funny.

At least their driver seemed to know how to weave in and out of traffic and give plenty of hand signals and blow the horn to navigate with the rest of the vehicles.

So, Christina sat back in the seat and stared out at the beautiful lights of the city glistening like colorful stars. When they pulled up to their hotel she saw that the lights reflected in the river as clearly as in a mirror. It all looked very magical.

"Can we go see the pyramids tonight?" she asked hopefully.

Mimi said, "No."

Papa said, "Yes."

Grant said, *"Min faDlak!"* which he had somehow learned was Arabic for "please."

The driver chose from all those answers and did not stop at the hotel but kept on speeding by and traveling down one road and another until suddenly Christina spied the most magical sight of all—the pyramids glowing golden in the night.

"Woooooow!" said Grant, marveling at the view.

"Can we go see them, please?" begged Christina.

This time it was neither Mimi nor Papa who answered, for they were staring open-mouthed at the amazing sight of the pyramids themselves.

Instead, their driver chuckled and said in perfectly good English, "Oh, no, little ones! It is time for you to get to bed after your long trip. Tomorrow is soon enough for you to explore the only one of the Seven Wonders of the Ancient World to survive. Besides, at night, the tomb robbers might get you!" He chuckled even louder this time, then made a U-turn and sped back toward the hotel.

"Tomb robbers?" Grant whispered to Christina in the back seat. "Is he kidding?"

"I hope so," said Christina, also in a low voice. "But who knows? Welcome to civilization, little brother. I don't think we're in Kansas anymore!"

"We don't live in Kansas," Grant grumbled.

"It's just an expression, Grant," explained his sister. "It's from the movie *The Wizard of Oz*."

"Well I don't see any Tin Man or Scarecrow or Cowardly Lion or..." Grant said.

"Grant..." said his sister, "just forget it!"

Walk Like An Egyptian

After a quick dinner sent up by room service, Grant and Christina were more than happy to get tucked in their beds. Papa said goodnight and headed off for his newspapers.

Mimi, in a pretty, silk caftan, sat on the end of Christina's bed. She always liked to hang around before bedtime and tell them things about their new destination, sort of like the lady with the 1,001 stories, Christina thought. Tonight was no different.

"You know," Mimi began, "the country of Egypt really flourished from 3000 BCE to 30 BCE. During that time more than 30 dynasties came and went."

"Is that when the pyramids were built?" Grant asked, snuggling down under the covers.

"Oh, yes," said Mimi, "and many other things, too.   Great temples, pyramids, statues, and more. The Egyptians were very creative in many ways. They created tales about gods and how things came to be."

"That's called mythology, right?" asked Christina. "We studied that in school last year."

"Correct!" said Mimi proudly.   "And they invented a unique system of writing called..."

"I know that!" cried Grant.   **"Hieroglyphs!** Remember, we saw the Rosetta stone in London and Papa gave you that necklace with your name written in **hieroglyphs** for your birthday."

Mimi winked and pulled down the neck of her caftan to reveal the necklace. Christina admired the black cord strung with bronze-colored figures of birds and other shapes.

"That's right," Mimi said.   "The Rosetta Stone helped people translate what the **hieroglyphs** said."

"They cracked the code!" said Grant.

"And people have been discovering Ancient Egypt for many years and are still searching for answers to many of the myths and mysteries of the past," finished Mimi.

"That sounds spooky, Mimi," said Christina, feeling a chill even beneath the thick covers.

"Well, things like mummies, and curses, and tombs, and tomb raiders always sound spooky, don't they?" Mimi teased.

Then she got a very serious look on her face.

"What's wrong, Mimi?" Christina asked. "Is it about what happened at the airport today?"

Her grandmother sighed. "I have to admit it is," she answered softly. "I had hoped to have a pleasant vacation this trip and not work on any mysteries in spite of what I said earlier, but..."

"But what?!" her grandchildren interrupted her.

In a moment of weakness, Mimi confessed. "Those plans that were stolen were about a newly-discovered gravesite. The archaeologists were hoping to excavate peacefully, but there always seem to be people with other ideas."

"Like what?" asked Grant.

"Oh, like robbing the tombs for valuables before they are excavated," said Mimi.

"Are there mummies in those tombs?" asked Christina. She had her fingers crossed behind her back, not really knowing if she wanted her grandmother to answer "Yes" or "No."

Mimi gave Christina a curious look. "Of course there are," she said. "That's why they are tombs. But there may also be gold and jewels and other valuables. And, something even more important."

"What's that?" Grant asked. Christina knew he figured gold and jewels were important enough.

"History!" answered Mimi. "History and answers are lurking in those tombs."

"So can we go and visit those tombs?" asked Christina eagerly.

"Oh, I doubt that," said Mimi. "But we can visit the pyramids at Giza tomorrow...IF you two behave yourselves."

"I promise!" said Grant. He hopped out of bed and stood there. "I promise...I promise...I even promise to walk like an Egyptian," he said.

Mimi laughed and stood up. "Grant, I don't even know what that means!"

Then Grant surprised both Mimi and Christina by doing a stiff-legged, bent-armed dance while bobbing his head back and forth. They laughed at Grant's antics.

"Okay, I think I get the idea," said Mimi. "Now

you get to bed!"

As Grant climbed back into bed and Mimi turned out the lights, Christina snuggled down into the covers and thought to herself...*I plan to think like an Egyptian and solve this mystery before anything can disappear, or anyone can get hurt...and Mimi and Papa will never even know what I'm up to!*

Piles of Pyramids

"Hey, Christina," Grant whispered the next morning before it was even daylight. "Do you know what King Tut said when he had a tummy ache?"

Christina put her head under the covers. Her brother's jokes were always so lame, but she knew he would not leave her alone until she answered. "No, Grant, what did King Tut say?" she gave in and asked.

"I WANT MY MUMMY!"

Grant chortled away while Christina groaned and slid further under the covers.

"Hey, let's get up!" said Grant. "Today is go-to-the-pyramids day!"

"Hey, that's right!" said Christina, jumping out of bed and dashing into the bathroom first and slamming the door.

"No fair!" screamed Grant. "You tricked me! I'm gonna put a curse on you!" He banged on the door to no avail. Poor Grant!

Once they were dressed, Christina and Grant left Mimi and Papa sleeping and slipped out of the room and headed for the elevator.

"Everything looks so...so...so..." Grant began.

"So Egyptian?" finished Christina.

"Yeah!" said Grant. "All this Oriental carpet, or whatever it is, and this marble and gold, and these little bugs crawling around everywhere?"

"Yikes!" squealed Christina. "What bugs?"

Grant pointed to decorations along the walls and on the doors.

"Oh," said Christina. "Those are scarabs."

"You mean like when I scrape my knee and it heals up into a scab?" Grant asked. He was always scraping his knees, usually when riding (or rather, falling off) his skateboard.

"Not scab," Christina corrected him. "Scarab. A scarab is a...a..."

"A scarab is the sacred dung beetle of ancient

Egypt," a boy's voice called from behind them.

Grant and Christina both gasped and turned. A few steps behind them stood an Egyptian boy about Christina's age, and an Egyptian girl about Grant's age.

"You often see jewelry made in a scarab design from beautiful gems," the girl added.

Christina and Grant were speechless for a moment. Each stood there with their mouths hanging open with a million questions.

"Who are you?" asked Christina. It was still dark outside and she might not have been surprised to see a few other early-bird adults up, but not children.

The boy bowed and the girl curtsied, which further surprised Christina and Grant.

"I am Farouk," said the boy.

"I am Suzanne," said the girl.

Christina thought the two children looked like models with their beautiful tan skin, black hair, and dark eyes. She figured they were brother and sister since they favored one another so much.

"I'm Christina," Christina said.

"I'm Grant; what's dung?"

Christina was so embarrassed. But the

question did not seem to bother Farouk who answered, "Dung is animal poop." When Christina looked surprised at his answer, the boy added, "I have been to America and watch CNN...I know some of your slang."

"So you make jewelry out of animal poop?" said Grant, looking very puzzled. He screwed his nose up. "This is a very strange country."

Farouk laughed. "Wait till you hear how we pull the brain out through the nose!" he said proudly.

Grant backed away. Suzanne punched her brother on the shoulder. "Oh, Farouk," she said. "Don't be mean and tease so. These are our guests; be nice." But she giggled anyway and when Christina looked puzzled she added, "It's true. One way the ancient Egyptians removed the brain before mummification was to take a long needle up into the nose and..."

"STOP! STOP!" cried Grant, holding two X-crossed fingers in his "curse" pose. "Too much information. I haven't even had breakfast yet."

"Then breakfast will be our treat!" said Farouk.

Suzanne nodded and explained, "Our father is

the manager of this hotel. He told us you were coming and we should be prepared to treat you like favored guests."

"That's really nice!" said Christina. "But why treat us so special? How does your father even know us?"

Suzanne laughed. "He knows we read your Mimi's mysteries," she confided. "We hope she might put us in one of her books."

Grant stroked his foot back and forth on the carpet and twisted his head one way and another. "Ohhhh, I don't know about that," he said. "Mimi is pretttttty picky when it comes to choosing book characters."

Farouk and Suzanne looked sad, then confused when Christina started laughing at them. "Grant is teasing you now," she said. "I'm sure Mimi would love to put you in a book once she meets you, especially if Grant and I beg her to!"

"*Pssst, pssst!*" hissed Grant. "There is NO new mystery book set in Egypt, remember?" he reminded his sister.

Once more, Suzanne and Farouk looked crestfallen.

Christina sighed. "Grant's just saying that,"

she said, "because Mimi always says that she's not writing a mystery...but it's never true."

"What's not true?" a voice called from down the hall. It was their grandmother. Mimi stuck her curly blond head out the door and reached down to pick up the newspaper.

"Nothing, Mimi!" her grandchildren called after her.

"We're on the way to breakfast with our new friends, Farouk and Suzanne." The two children bowed and curtsied yet again.

Mimi waved and yawned and said, "Okay, see you there," then turned and closed the door. All the kids watched in surprise as the decorative scarab holding the door number clattered to the carpet along with a piece of paper.

"What's that?" asked Christina. Grant was already running to retrieve the paper, which he unfolded and read.

"A clue!" he called back to the others.

"No way," said Christina.

"Hurray, hurray!" said Farouk and his sister together. "A mystery book clue!"

Christina stalked back down the hall. She would never get to eat breakfast at this rate, she thought, and knew she had to put a stop to all this mystery silliness right away. She grabbed the note out of her brother's hand and read it. Then she thrust the note under Farouk's nose and asked in an irritated voice, "What does that word say?"

Farouk took the note and looked at it. All the writing was in English except for one word which was in **hieroglyphs.**

Farouk looked at Christina and began reading. "It says:

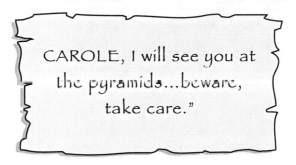

CAROLE, I will see you at the pyramids...beware, take care."

No Clue?

Christina felt the tiny hairs on the back of her arms stand up. "That does not sound like a clue," she said. "That sounds like a threat! And I don't like anyone threatening my grandmother, and neither will Papa when he hears about this!" She grabbed the door knob to open the door but Grant stopped her.

"Wait, Christina!" he said. "Don't worry Mimi. Maybe it's a joke. Maybe it's one of her researcher or photographer friends. We can keep an eye out for her. But if it's a clue, we want to keep it for ourselves, don't we?"

Christina looked doubtful, but Farouk and Suzanne were whispering, "Yes, yes, let's keep the clue!"

Grant looked at his sister pleadingly.

"Pleeeeease?"

"Oh, ok," Christina said, dropping her hand from the door knob. "But this is no clue, I'm sure. If you guys want a mystery, you'll have to try harder than that."

"HEY!" cried a voice from down the hall. A head of wild white hair stuck out of a doorway. The old man glared up and down the hallway. "Who's making all that noise?"

Quickly, the kids began to tiptoe away down the hall. Just as they got to the elevator, Grant turned and said to the man, "No clue, sir, no clue!"

At breakfast in the fabulous dining room, Grant and Christina told their new friends about the events at the airport and how they were worried that the man had seen and could recognize them.   Christina figured that Farouk and Suzanne would just make fun of them or reassure them that they were only letting their imaginations run away with them and that there was nothing to worry about.

So, Christina was surprised when Farouk said, "Then you should be worried, I think. After all, number one, grave robbing is a very serious offense in Egypt, but some people think that it is worth the risk to steal valuables from the tombs. After all, number two, you two stick out like a sore thumb here with your blond hair, fair skin, and big blue eyes."

But Suzanne had a different take on the matter. "Oh, don't worry," she said. "Just have fun with us. Enjoy your trip. I do not think anything bad will happen to you or your Mimi while you are here."

Christina had been enjoying her breakfast of eggs, *aish* (bread), and apricot juice, but all this talk frightened her.

Grant had been ignoring the discussion and stuffed something dark on his plate into his mouth. "Yuck!" he said. "That taste like beetle dung...what was it?"

The kids looked at his empty plate and empty mouth and laughed.

"Since you have already eaten whatever it is, you do not need to know!" said Farouk with a grin. He and his sister knew that it was just a date.

The girls laughed but Grant frowned and wiped his mouth with a napkin as if he could rub away the taste.

"Tell us about the pyramids at Giza," said Christina, changing the subject. "I hope we'll be going there soon."

Farouk's eyes lit up and Christina could tell that he loved to talk about his native country and knew its history well.

"When you go to Giza today, you will be traveling back in Egyptian history to the time of the pharaohs. At Giza, that would be about 5,000 years ago. That's about when Giza became the royal burial ground for dead kings."

"So you mean, Giza's one big cemetery?" asked Christina.

"Yes," said Suzanne, eager to get in her say. "The dead kings were brought there to be buried beneath, or sometimes inside, the pyramids."

"So you mean the pyramids are really tombs?" asked Grant.

When both Farouk and Suzanne nodded, Grant said, "Oh, now I get it; grave robbers, tomb robbers, no wonder I keep hearing that. But why do people just want to collect a bunch of skeletons?"

Farouk and Suzanne looked at one another in puzzlement.

"They are not after the bodies—usually," said Farouk. "They are after the gold!"

"Gold?" Grant asked. "GOLD?!"

Gold!

"Of course," said Suzanne, explaining. "Kings were buried with all the things that they would need in the afterlife. That might mean gold, dishes, even pets and servants."

"Wow," said Grant, "I think I'd rather be a king! But what good would all that stuff be in the afterlife when you were just a pile of dust?"

The other three children stared at Grant over their breakfast dishes. Grant stared back. He knew they thought he should know the answer, and then suddenly, it came to him.

"MUMMIES!" he said. "They got made into mummies, right?"

"Right, Grant," said Christina, "but not so loud. You talk loud enough to wake the dead."

"Do not talk about the dead with disrespect,"

Farouk warned her.

Christina looked offended. "I never do," she said. Then she calmed down a bit. Mimi always said, "when in Rome do as the Romans do," which meant that when you were a visitor in a country, you should look and listen and not be a know-it-all or be offended by something when you might not even know what someone meant.

"I see that the car is waiting for us," Farouk said.

"Let's go," said Grant. "Hey, do you know what kind of underwear King Tut wears?"

Suzanne looked at Grant like he was crazy. "No, what kind?" she asked.

"Fruit of the Tomb!" said Grant.

Christina frowned and the other two kids did not laugh. Christina thought that now it was their turn to explain something that got lost in the translation.

When Farouk and Suzanne looked at her for an explanation to what Grant obviously meant as a joke, she said, "You probably have to be American to get it...or watch a lot of Saturday morning cartoons."

Before the kids could stew over the matter further, Papa appeared at the entrance to the dining room and beckoned for them to hurry up. And before they knew it, they were out in the bright Egyptian morning headed for the Giza plateau to see the famous Pyramids of Giza.

For some reason, Christina had pictured the Giza plateau as a lonesome endless swath of hills of sand surrounding three large pyramids with the famous Sphinx guarding them.

However, when they arrived at Giza, it was more like a circus! True, the pyramids were amazing...and there was plenty of sand. But there were also taxis, tour buses, camels, tented stalls with people selling souvenirs and food, and tourists, tourists, tourists.

Nonetheless, in a moment, Christina gazed at the Sphinx and pyramids and put all the other distractions aside in her mind. Quickly, she was transported back in time to the era of kingdoms and pharaohs, and magical construction feats such as the pyramids.

"Boy, howdy!" said Papa in his cowboy drawl. "How did they build these things way back then?" Papa was always interested in engineering, roads, bridges, and everything that required a tool or a horse.

Their guide, Wazee, said, "It is amazing, no? These awesome pyramids were built in less than 100 years. The Great Pyramid," he said, pointing toward it, "is the oldest and largest, built by the king of the 4th **Dynasty** of the Old Kingdom, Khufu. And Abu al-Hol guards them all."

"Abu who?" asked Grant.

"The guardian of the Giza plateau called the Father of Terror by Arabs," Wazee explained. "What you call The Sphinx."

"What are the pyramids made of?" asked Mimi, wiping her brow with a scarf. It was already warm, even this early, on the plateau.

Wazee looked pleased to explain. "The Great Pyramid is made of more than two million blocks of stone. Each stone weighs about two and one-half tons! A few of the base stones weigh 15 tons each! Until the 19th century, it was the tallest structure in the world."

"But how did they build the pyramids way back then," Christina marveled, "before bulldozers and cranes and things like that?"

"Ahhhh," said Wazee, his turban bobbing.

"That is a mystery, no? At first the pyramids were built of mudbrick *mastabas* shaped sort of like a gold brick. Later, the *mastabas* were stacked into pyramids that looked like steps. Even later, these steps were filled in to create a smooth-sided pyramid. Those Egyptians, they were very ingenious," he added proudly.

"What I want to know is what's inside of the Great Pyramid?" said Papa. He stared out into the desert, his cowboy hat tilted back on his head. Sweat glistened in beads on his brow. His nose and cheeks were red, even though Mimi had slathered them all with plenty of white, gooey sunblock.

"The King's Chamber," said Wazee, "where he was buried. But, of course, tomb robbers broke in and stole anything of value many, many years ago."

"Can we go closer?" asked Christina.

"Can we go inside?" Grant asked eagerly. Mimi frowned.

Wazee did not speak. He merely nodded and camels appeared for them all to ride upon. Mimi frowned even more.

"It is easy," promised Wazee. "I will help you."

Soon, they all were aboard camels, and now Christina could understand why they were called Ships of the Desert as they rolled from side to side across the sand. She held on for dear life!

They were silent as they rode along and Christina felt like she was in some magical fairytale. As they approached the pyramids, she could easily imagine ancient Egyptian workers hard at work in the hot desert, kings dressed for death in gold and jewels, and beautiful queens with dark black hair, exotic makeup, and dramatic outfits.

Of course, then her camel spoiled the fairytale moment by deciding to have a sneezing, spitting fit which bumped her up and down and back into reality. Grant laughed with glee until his camel started the same antics and he had to hold on for dear life!

When they dismounted, Wazee led them into a door and inside the pyramid. "This would not be for the claustrophobic," he said of the narrow passageways.

"That would be me," said Mimi, but she continued on. Mimi was always a good sport and not about to give up and be left behind on any adventure.

Suzanne and Farouk had stayed behind to visit the stalls, saying that they had been in the pyramids many times.

Inside the pyramid, it was hot and airless, and their visit was much shorter than Grant and Christina would have liked. They looked around at the chambers and marveled at the construction. But soon, Wazee led them back outside into the bright sunshine and fresh—though hot—air.

Wazee gave them all bottles of chilled water. He told Papa, "The pyramids were once covered with limestone but later rulers took it off to use for their own monuments. And once it was a great hobby for tourists to climb the pyramids."

"Can we climb one?!" Grant asked excitedly.

"Too dangerous," said Mimi.

"Too hot," said Papa.

"No longer allowed," said Wazee.

"Too bad," said Grant in disappointment.

Christina was not saying anything. She had walked to her camel and found a note tucked under the harness. While no one was looking, she unfolded it and read:

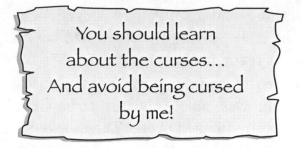

You should learn
about the curses...
And avoid being cursed
by me!

Christina looked around. Now the area was filled with even more tourists and camels and drivers and others, and she could not spot any young man who looked like the one she had seen in the airport. She swallowed hard and felt sand in her teeth and throat, and a gritty sort of fear in her heart.

A Curse?
Of Course!

Soon, they were back at the hotel in the cool and shady outdoor café, drinking tall glasses of lemonade with tangy leaves of mint floating on the ice.

They sat at a large round table with a billowy white table cloth. Two colorful parasols tilted above them overhead. The café was surrounded by tinkling fountains, palm trees, and other beautiful greenery.

Everyone was talking about the exciting morning at the pyramids except Christina. Even Wazee had joined them, at Papa's request, since he was taking them to the Egyptian Museum that afternoon.

Finally, Christina could contain herself no longer. "Is there really a curse?" she blurted out right in the middle of a conversation everyone was having on a completely different subject.

"Christina!" Mimi said. "You know we don't believe in any such thing as curses."

Wazee had a strange look on his face. "Of course," he said to Mimi, his head lowered in deference, "you have heard of the famous Curse of the Pharoahs?"

"Of course," Mimi admitted.

"Tell us! Tell us!" Grant and Christina shouted together.

Farouk raised his hand as if he were in a classroom. "I can tell!"

All eyes fell on him and he began. "Some people say that there is a curse associated with the tomb of King Tutankhamun. After his tomb was opened, it is said that a famous English lord died. Some writing in the tomb was translated as 'I will kill all of those who cross this threshold.'"

Christina and Grant gasped. The adults just listened patiently. Suzanne hid a secret smile behind her hand.

Farouk continued: "From then on, anything

bad that happened related to the famous king's tomb was blamed on the curse."

"Well I don't believe all that," Suzanne interrupted. "Later, that same writing was translated into something like 'I am the one who prevents the sand from blocking the secret chamber.' That doesn't sound like a curse at all."

That made Papa and Mimi laugh. Christina was still uncertain as to what to believe, but she did not want to tell anyone about the note yet. Papa would say she liked to play her cards close to her vest.

Wazee said, "If you focus on the curse, you miss out on one of the most exciting moments in archaeological history!" He pulled a tattered book from his pocket and began to read aloud:

"At first I could see nothing, the hot air escaping from the chamber causing the candle flame to flicker, but presently, as my eyes grew accustomed to the light, details of the room within emerged slowly from the mist, strange animals, statues and gold—everywhere the glint of gold.

"Those are the words of the famous archaeologist Howard Carter as he entered the never-before-seen tomb of Tutankhamun," Wazee explained. "Can you imagine the excitement?!"

"It is hard to imagine," Christina admitted.

"Even today it is very exciting when a new find is made," said Farouk. "For example, in the ancient Valley of the Kings!"

Suzanne elected to tell this tale. "One day, a donkey stumbled in a hole in the sand. It turned out to be over the tombs of hundreds, maybe even thousands and thousands, of mummies!"

"Wow!" said Grant. "Egypt must have mummies buried on every street corner. It seems like you have enough for everyone to have a mummy."

"It seems that way sometimes," Farouk said with a sigh, "but do not tease about taking mummies. It is a crime."

Mimi stood up. "Well, perhaps we should stop talking about mummies—and curses—and go and see some mummies for ourselves?"

"Yes!" said Christina

"Oh, yes, grandmummy," said Grant with a giggle.

"Let's go or I'll put a curse on you both!" promised Papa.

Eenie, Meenie, Mummy, Mo

As Wazee let them out at the entrance to the Egyptian Museum, Christina and Grant were very excited. After all the talk about mummies, they wanted to see some up-close-and-personal for themselves.

Mimi and Papa liked to tour a museum from start to finish, while their grandchildren liked to dash around and see everything they could— especially the most exciting things first.

Farouk and Suzanne suggested that they head for the Tutankhamun Galleries first. Wazee said he was going to get the car washed, but the kids thought his sleepy-looking eyes really meant he would go and take a nap.

In the Tutankhamun Galleries, the kids marveled over the life-sized gold death mask of the famous boy king. Christina and Grant had not realized that he was only 19 years old when he died, and that he had a wife.

"There's so much gold!" said Christina. "Just look at this throne." The king's throne had golden lion heads and legs on each side.

They looked over everything from beds and jewelry to hunting knives and board games— everything a king might need in the afterlife. There were even 413 little statues of the king that were supposed to help him in the afterlife; one for each day of the year and extras to supervise them.

"This is all very strange," admitted Christina.

"It was a long time ago and people believed different things," said Farouk.

"Where is King Tut now?" asked Grant, looking around suspiciously.

"Oh, don't worry," said Suzanne. "His body is in its tomb in the Valley of the Kings on the west bank of the Nile River."

"But if you want to see mucho mummies," said Farouk teasingly, "Follow me!"

Farouk led them to the Royal Mummy Room in a different part of the museum. Much to Grant's and Christina's amazement, there were indeed many mummies. They were arranged around the room. They could hardly believe that these mummified remains were of people who had lived more than 3,000 years ago.

Everyone moved along to view the bodies in a respectful silence. Christina could tell that Grant was pretty much speechless. He had dressed up as a mummy one Halloween when their Mom bound him up in strips of sheet from head to toe. He was very realistic-looking, and Trick-or-Treated until he had to go to the bathroom and so had to get u n w o u n d!

The dark brown faces and shredded skin made Christina think of people who might have smoked themselves to death, but she knew that was not true.

"How do they mummify people?" she whispered to Farouk.

"Let's take a break and I will explain," he whispered back.

Christina nodded and the children filed out of the room, tugging Grant along behind them.

They went out into a courtyard and sat on a low stone bench.

"The ancient Egyptians believed in an afterlife," said Farouk. "When someone died, they mummified them so that their body would be preserved for all eternity to hold their soul. They also buried them with all the things they might need in the afterlife, sometimes including animals."

"You can mummify animals?" asked Grant.

"Sure," said Suzanne. "Some animals and people got naturally mummified just by being in sand graves. The sand sucked out all the moisture in their bodies and left them mummies."

"But later," said Farouk, "people used something called *natron* to dry out bodies in 40 days. They removed all the internal organs, except the heart, and put them in jars to save with the body. Then they embalmed the body, dried it out with natron, and wrapped the body in linen."

"Sounds like a beauty shop for dead folks," said Grant with a grimace. "I would not like that job."

"So next they put the bodies in coffins?"

asked Christina.

"Yes," said Farouk. "And a famous king like Tutankhamun had several coffins, then a sarcophagus."

"A what?" asked Grant.

"A sarcophagus is a burial vault," said Suzanne. "And then kings were put in tombs often guarded by other mummies."

"Creepy," said Grant.

"No," said Christina, *"that's* creepy!" She pointed to a man coming out of the museum. He wore a mask.

"Oh, lots of mummies had death masks," said Farouk. "That was so the dead person's spirit could find its body."

Christina looked suspiciously at the man in jeans, a tee shirt, and the mask. "But why is HE wearing one. You don't think?..."

Before she could finish her sentence, the boy took off running and jumped right over the wall! He held a package under one arm, which he carried like a football.

Alarms suddenly sounded and the children jumped up.

Armed security guards dashed out of the building and over the wall after the man.

"I can't believe someone actually just tried to steal ancient artifacts from the famous Egyptian Museum!" said Farouk.

"I'd say he's stolen them," Grant corrected.

"What's this?" said Suzanne. She bent down and picked up a white note from beneath the bench right where Christina had been sitting. "I think the thief dropped this right in your lap before you jumped up, Christina."

Christina took the note and opened it. It read:

We meet again. Can you catch a thief?
Are you really that brave?

Suddenly, other people ran out into the courtyard.

"He stole a mask!" one person shouted.

"He stole a cat mummy!" shouted another.

"It's an outrage!" shouted a third.

"He is dangerous—I saw a gun!" cried a fourth person.

Suzanne turned to Christina. "It seems you have a dangerous, gun-toting (as you would say in America) new friend. This cannot be a good thing, no?"

Christina hung her head. "No," she admitted. She did not want to be considered friends with a thief. In fact, it made her very angry. She stomped her foot in the sand. More than one can play cops and robbers and cat and mouse and put curses on people, she thought to herself. She said to Suzanne in a firm voice, "It is the thief who had better look out and beware!"

Nile, Nile, Crocodile

The next morning, Christina and Grant were delighted to find that they were going on a trip down the famous Nile River! Of course, this did mean that they would no longer be around Cairo to keep up with the Great Cat Caper. However, it did mean that they would get to visit the famous Valley of the Kings.

Early, Christina and Mimi went out to one of the many bazaars to shop for a few things that her grandmother thought they needed for the trip. As they traipsed through shops, Christina marveled at the curious variety of wonderful and strange things for sale.

There were Queen Nefertiti reading lamps,

sheesha (waterpipes), papyrus, all kinds of copper pots, camel-hair rugs, beautiful silk scarves, belly-dancing outfits, gold and silver jewelry, and spices galore—many bright enough to use as paints!

Christina especially liked the many little jewel-colored perfume bottles with fancy glass stoppers. When Mimi wasn't looking, she bought her grandmother a lavender and green bottle for a souvenir. She also bought Grant a small backgammon board, hoping they might get to play while they were sailing down the Nile.

Mimi loved to buy souvenirs and swore Christina to secrecy when she bought Papa a fancy glass and bronze waterpipe for his desk and herself a red and gold belly-dancing costume.

As they worked their way through the shops, sometimes the tiny streets in between would twist and turn in a maze of color and noise and smells. All at once, Christina realized that she and her grandmother were no longer together. Try as she might to backtrack and catch up, she could not find Mimi. For a time, she was not too worried, but after reaching several dead-ends, Christina grew more nervous, then afraid.

At first, Christina thought that the sights

were wonderful and exotic. But now they grew eerie and outlandish in her fear. She realized that she could not read the Arabic street signs so she had no idea where she was. The tall minarets of the **mosques** seemed to grow like something in an Alice in Wonderland story until she felt smaller and smaller. As the maze of streets grew narrower and narrower and Christina spied no other tourists, she felt like she might cry.

Suddenly, she turned a corner and in her rush knocked over a stall on wheels which sent fruits and vegetables tumbling everywhere. She cried, "*min faDlah, law samaHt,*" hoping she was saying, "Excuse me!" but not sure.

When she turned again, almost falling down, a man's arms lifted her from the pavement. When Christina looked up through her tears she felt sure she saw the thief! As he held her tightly and gave her an evil "Gotcha!" smile, Christina yanked from his grasp and ran down the path as fast as she could.

All of a sudden, she found herself on a main street in front of a coffee shop with an outdoor patio. There sat Mimi, who looked relieved to see her granddaughter. "Thank goodness!"

Mimi said. "We got separated and I couldn't find you. I thought maybe if I stayed put a few minutes, you might find me and you did."

Christina fell into Mimi's arms.

"Are you alright?" Mimi asked her. "Are you scared, hurt?"

"No, no," Christina said, shaking her head. "Just out of breath." She knew that if she told her grandmother what had just happened, well, for one thing, she could not prove it was the bad guy...and for another, Mimi would call Papa and the police and they would never make the afternoon departure on their trip.

As Christina sat down in a chair and Mimi ordered her a *wajbah khafeefah* (snack), she calmed down. Putting her napkin in her lap, Christina thought the best thing that they could do was to leave Cairo for a few days. But that didn't keep her from looking around nervously for any sight of the thief.

Late that afternoon, Mimi, Papa, Grant and Christina arrived at the dock to board the *felucca* for their trip. Christina thought the ancient sailing boats with their pointed white sails were beautiful. She was just sorry that Farouk and Suzanne had school and could not join them. They promised to watch the news and see if the Mummy Cat Thief was caught. Christina was at least relieved that she was leaving her unwanted new "friend" behind in Cairo. He might look for her, but he would not find her if she were on the Nile.

"Mimi, you actually packed light," Papa marveled.

"We all did," Mimi promised.

When the loading was done, they set sail just in time to enjoy the beautiful sunset.

As they sailed out of the harbor, the captain explained that Egypt was often described as the "gift of the Nile," because without the river, the country would just be a barren desert.

"We've traveled up and down the Mississippi River in America," Christina shared. "We learned then what a difference a river makes."

The captain smiled and nodded. His bright teeth glowed pink in the reflection of the setting sun. "The *fellaheen* farm today much as they did in ancient Egypt," he said. "Once the annual flooding brought fresh silt out onto the land.

After the Aswan High Dam was built, the flooding stopped, but not the farming."

He told them they would see mudbrick villages where the farmers lived. But what Christina and Grant were excited about was to visit some of the famous ancient Egyptian monuments that lined the river.

Everyone grew quiet and lazy as the *felucca* darted among other boats. Soon, a picnic dinner of lentil soup and *mezzes* of *hummus* and *babaghanoush* was served. There was watermelon for dessert and Christina and Grant had a seed-spitting contest until Mimi made them settle down.

Papa had brought sleeping bags for them and the two kids snuggled down beneath the moon and stars to dream of Egypt long ago. And when they awoke to blue sky and bright sun, they were at the famous Egyptian historical site—Luxor, in the Valley of the Kings!

When Christina rubbed her eyes and sat up and looked out on the water, the first thing she saw was a crocodile!

Unlucky Luxor

Christina was fascinated. The banks of the Nile River were lush with greenery of all types. Beyond...was the desert. Her teacher would say Egypt was a land of contrasts: old and new; ancient and modern. And, to Christina, most mysterious.

To replenish their provisions, they visited a market. The *souk* was filled with beautiful fresh vegetables. Grant had to jump out of the way of a donkey cart! Once more, Christina enjoyed looking at the bright, colorful containers of spices. One spice was bright blue!

"Wow! Look at that castle," Grant cried, pointing to a large mass of buildings and colonnades.

"That is the Temple of Luxor," the captain

explained.   "It was built by the pharaoh Amenhotep III in the 18th century. In the 19th century, Ramses II added to it. Even Alexander the Great made improvements to Luxor Temple."

"Boy, that is historic...and old!" said Grant.

"Aha!" said the captain. "But what you see here was once abandoned and covered in silt and sand for 1,000 years. Then, like most everything else in Egypt, it was 'rediscovered' by archaeologists...who had to move a village out of the temple before they could restore it."

Soon, they were in a caleche, rumbling down the Corniche. But before they got to the temple, the driver let them out so that they could walk down the avenue of sphinxes which led to the temple.

"One sphinx, two sphinx, red sphinx, blue sphinx," Grant muttered as he passed each ancient sculpture.

Christina was flabbergasted by the two gigantic colossi (statues) of Ramses that guarded the entrance to the temple. They all stared up at a pink granite obelisk.

"That looks familiar, Mimi," Christina said. "But how could it be familiar to me? I have never been to Egypt!"

"But you've been to Paris!" said Mimi. "The matching obelisk that once stood here now stands at the Place de la Concorde. It was a gift from Egypt."

"Gee," said Papa. "They have enough ancient ruins to give some away?"

"Well," said Mimi. "Maybe giving away your precious heritage isn't too smart, but neither is it too smart for other countries to claim it or for robbers to steal it."

"Other countries?" Christina asked, confused.

"Oh, yes," said Mimi. "It was once common for archaeologists to come to countries with wonderful ruins, like Greece and Rome...then cart off some of the best pieces. Some have been returned. Some are still being argued over."

"That might be like someone coming to paint the Statue of Liberty, then taking Lady Liberty's torch back home with them for a souvenir," Christina said.

Mimi laughed. "That's not a bad description. Remember that many historic ruins are priceless. Sometimes, people just couldn't help themselves.   But outright grave-robbing—well, that's something else."

All the talk about raiding tombs and stealing made Christina think harder than she wanted to about the man at the airport and the Cat Mummy Thief. Now it seemed that everywhere she looked she spotted a suspicious character who looked just like the man who had accosted her at the market in Cairo. But, surely, she thought, she was just letting her imagination get away with her again.

As they entered Luxor Temple, Christina realized that she hadn't seen anything yet!

"No wonder a whole village of people could live in the temple," said Grant. "This place is huge!"

For a while, the group paraded through endless courts, halls, and inner temples. Soon, Christina realized that she had made a wrong turn and had gotten separated from the others. In a panic, she looked all around, wondering how to find them. When a man's voice suddenly said, "This way," Christina spun around and was surprised to see no one. She began to run and was just as surprised to spy Mimi, Papa, and Grant heading out of the temple.

"You look like you've seen a ghost," Grant teased his sister.

Christina, pale and sweating in the warm sun, just nodded. "Maybe I heard one," she muttered to herself. "But I sure hope not!"

The Amazing Karnak

As much as they hated to leave Luxor Temple, they had to. Mimi said there was much more to see. Christina was getting the impression that Egypt was one big archaeological dig—with ancient ruins, mummies, and other historic artifacts pretty much everywhere!

After a quick lunch of grape leaves stuffed with rice and vegetables, they headed for Karnak.

"I am the Amazing Karnak!" Grant said over and over as they walked. Grant loved magic tricks and was actually very good at them. He thought Karnak sounded like a good name for a magician.   Christina just wished a magician would come along and help her solve the odd assortment of mysteries that seemed to be unraveling behind her like a mummy's linens.

Karnak was an enormous complex.   There was the amazing Temple of Amun. They learned from a guide that more than 80,000 people once worked on the temple, started in the 11th **Dynasty**.

Like Luxor, the temple was buried beneath the sand for 1,000 years before being rediscovered.   It was clear that restoration continued...and probably always would.

"Hey, there's a dung beetle!" Grant warned Christina.

His sister bolted away, only to discover that Grant meant a large sculpture of a scarab. Everything, in fact, was supersize!

The Colossus of Ramses II stood in front of the Great Hypostyle Hall. Christina wandered among the 134 enormous columns, which made her feel as small as a beetle bug. Just as before, she soon discovered that she was deep in the cavernous hall and all alone.

Suddenly, a deep voice spoke to her. The speaker seemed to be hiding behind a nearby column.

"Do not move!" he warned. "Little Miss Archaeologist, it would be best if you discontinued your efforts to try to resolve anything that you deem mysterious. Egypt is a mysterious country. You must let us resolve our own mysteries."

Christina froze in place. "I don't know what you are talking about," she said in a quivering voice. "I think you should leave me alone," she bravely added.

"This is a warning!" the voice said. "I would not want to see your grandmummy get mummificd."

"You should not threaten me," blurted Christina. "I'm just a kid and my Papa will be very angry when I tell him. He is not afraid of anything."

"Curses!" the voice hissed. "He just may be afraid of curses."

"NO!" Christina blared. "Papa does not believe in curses. And if you try to mummify Mimi you will be in big trouble."

"Aha!" said the voice. "Big trouble—that is what you and your bratty little brother are in. The Voice has spoken!"

Next, without a word of warning, Christina heard footsteps scurry away through the great hall among the columns. She caught a glimpse of someone in a khaki-colored outfit dashing away.

Instead of being scared, now she was mad. Mad enough to solve the mystery, she hoped. But was one man after her, or two? Was one a wild, crazy, mad archaeologist? That's what this most recent culprit sounded (and looked like) to her. Was the other the double thief? And what was it all about? Were they related? And who was sending her clues?

Suddenly, a bony finger tapped her on the shoulder. Startled, she spun around.

"Grant!" she cried. "You scared me silly."

"Oh, you were already silly," Grant said. "But why do you looked scared?"

"Shhh," Christina warned him. "Some guy was whispering to me from behind the columns. He made me mad."

"I could kick him," Grant volunteered.

Christina smiled. She was proud her little brother was always ready to come to her defense.

"That's ok," she said. "I plan to get revenge

another way."

"Revenge?" a voice said behind them. "We'll have none of that!" It was Mimi. She had only heard part of their conversation and thought her grandkids were arguing.

Papa peeked out from behind a column. "BOO!" he said. "Do you believe this place? Did you see the Sacred Lake? There are a whole bunch of lioness-goddesses lined up over there in the desert. And there's an open-air museum. We could be here all day and all night."

Mimi shook her head. "We can't stay here all night," she said. "We have to go back to town and have dinner and see the belly dancers."

"Ok!" said Papa, turning quickly on his heels in the sand. "Phooey with all this ancient Egyptian priceless antiquities stuff—let's go to town."

Mimi frowned.

Christina giggled.

And Grant led the way, doing his best (meaning perfectly awful!) imitation of a belly dance all the way back to the temple entrance.

Belly Dancing

Christina discovered that she was thrilled to get back to the inn where they were staying and cool off in the shade with some refreshing mint tea.

Later, they dressed for dinner and went to a nice restaurant that looked like it was situated in the center of an ancient Egyptian oasis. The palm tree fronds blew in the breeze. Soft pink and blue lights lit up their trunks. Once more, Christina felt like she was in a fairytale land.

For dinner they had stuffed lamb, salad, vegetables, a cheese called *domiati*, and dessert of pistachio nuts, the honey-sweet pastry *baklawa*, and apricot juice.

"I'm stuffed," said Papa. He loved to try new and exotic foods.

Mimi had just nibbled at her plate.

Grant continued to crunch pistachios.

Christina enjoyed one last piece of the luscious *baklawa*.

Then, it was time for the belly dancing!

Christina wondered if this was a show that kids should see. When the dancers came out, they wore beautiful costumes. The fabrics were sheer and jewel-toned. Gold discs hung from the headdress, bodice, and low-slung waist of the costumes. Sequins glistened and Christina could see smiles behind the flimsy veils the dancers wore over their faces.

"Oo, la la!" said Papa.

"Behave!" whispered Mimi.

An announcer explained, "Dancing was important in Egyptian history. It was part of our ancient rituals and celebrations. And, now, I present..."

Suddenly, beautiful music began to play. Slowly, the dancers moved to the center and edges of the dance floor.

"What are those things in their hands?" Grant asked. "Dung beetles?"

"Castanets, Grant, hush," said Mimi.

"Are they going to dance on their bellies?"

"Hush, Grant!" said Christina and Papa.

Soon the music grew louder and faster and the lady dancers began to move and shake and wiggle. Their hips moved faster and faster until they were a blur. Christina did not see how they danced so fast. She figured it must take a lot of practice and be very good exercise.

When the dance was over, everyone applauded very loudly. Christina could see Mimi wiggling in her chair, trying to figure the dance out. But suddenly they were all surprised when a man took the dance floor.

"Is he going to belly dance?" Grant asked.

"HUSH!" said Mimi, Christina, and Papa.

The man wore a bright red, and green, and gold costume. He began to twirl and twirl and twirl and twirl and twirl and TWIRLTWIRLTWIRLTWIRL! Everyone went wild with applause.

"What is that?" Christina asked.

"That's a whirling dervish," Mimi explained.

"Wow!" said Grant. "That's a dance I think I could be good at."

"And knock over every table in the place doing it," teased Christina.

Just then, as if to prove her point, the

whirling dervish finished his performance by twirling so close to their table that his costume swirled over Christina's lap. When she looked down, she saw that the man had left a note in her lap on top of her napkin. Quickly, she palmed the note and put it in her pocket.

"Well, that was quite an evening!" said Papa. "Let's call it a night."

He and Mimi sauntered toward the door, stopping to compliment the dancers milling around the stage. Christina took that opportunity to show Grant the note.

"Is it a clue?" he asked.

"Looks like it," Christina said excitedly. "She held the paper close to the candle. At the top was a strange-looking eye. "I think that's called the Evil Eye," she said. "And that can't be good." She read the note aloud.

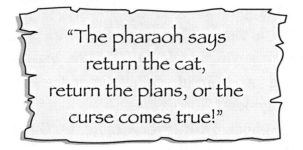

"The pharaoh says
return the cat,
return the plans, or the
curse comes true!"

"Wow!" said Grant. "Sounds like someone

thinks that we have those stupid plans that guy stole. And the mummy cat we saw the same guy or another guy steal. Why are they picking on us?"

"Good question," said Christina. "Perhaps a case of mistaken identity? But why would someone think that?"

"Maybe just because we were at both places when the thief struck? Maybe they think we're in cahoots with the thief?" Grant suggested.

"That's a lot of maybes," said Christina wearily. "And we can't even explain ourselves because we can't find anyone to explain to."

"You can explain to me," said a deep voice. It was Papa. He had returned for them. "You can explain why your grandmother and I are out at the carriage and you two are still here at the table."

"Sorry, Papa," said Christina. "I guess we were just daydreaming or something."

"More like exhausted, I imagine," said Papa, gently rubbing both their heads. "Let's go."

Slowly, they followed their grandfather out of the empty café. Christina knew that they would go back to the inn and get into bed. But she did not think she would be getting much sleep on this Evil Eye of a night!

Valley of the Kings

The next morning, the four tourists headed to Thebes in the Valley of the Kings. Grant was excited because that was where King Tut was buried, along with a lot of other ancient Egyptian pharaohs.

Christina held the map. "This looks like a street map with lots of dead ends," she said.

"Dead end is a good description," Mimi teased. "This is a necropolis, you know—a burial ground. The pharaohs got tired of having robbers ransack their tombs. They began to bury their dead here in these limestone hills in hopes that the tombs would be safely hidden deep in the mountains."

"I'll bet it did help," Grant speculated.

"Not at all," said Mimi. "All the tombs were robbed except a few, and one of those belonged to..."

Before her grandmother could finish her sentence, Christina interrupted her excitedly, "To Tutankhamun!"

"Exactly!" said Papa, joining the conversation.

Christina stared out at the barren landscape. "So if almost all of the 62 tombs were robbed, what are we here to see?"

"Oh, many of the burial chambers are still beautiful with art on the walls, **hieroglyphs**, and a sarcophagus or two," said Mimi.

After they bought tickets to visit the tombs, they sat down for a short rest in the hot sun. Everyone sipped from their water bottles and stared out at the enormous sand graveyard.

"Do you feel ok, Christina?" Mimi asked in a concerned voice. She pressed her palm on her granddaughter's forehead. "You feel warm."

Christina giggled. "It must be 90 degrees in the shade, Mimi," she reminded her grandmother. "I'd be sick if I felt cold. I'm ok, really. Let's go visit the dead people."

Grant groaned. His face was red and flushed. "Are we having fun yet?"

Papa laughed. "It isn't exactly Disney World, is it, buddy?"

Grant sighed. "I thought looking at raggedy mummified dead people would be fun, but when you've seen one I think you've seen them all. And we've seen more dead people than alive people in the last few days. I sure miss Farouk and Suzanne."

Papa was always full of motivational ideas. "Well, we don't want you to be bored in the middle of the most famous piece of civilization on earth, so how about you be in charge of the scorpions?"

"Scorpions?!" Mimi and Christina said together, looking all around the rocks where they sat and lifting up their feet and squiggling their toes in their sandals.

"Sure," said Papa. "Desert...scorpions. Just like in the western United States."

Now Grant could really sink his teeth into scorpions, if you know what I mean. "Sure," he agreed readily. "I'll be on Scorpion Guard. You silly ladies don't have to worry...I'm wearing my deadly stomping sandals and I will squash any scorps we see."

Papa grinned and marched off, Grant following, looking left and right at the sand as he took high steps. Mimi and Christina rolled their eyes and followed along behind. Christina figured if Grant saw a "scorp" as he had nicknamed the bugs, he would jump right into Papa's arms...and since Papa would have his arms full, she and Mimi would have to do the sandal stomping!

The tombs were actually much more interesting than Christina expected. She had brought her notebook and recorded the following:

•Tomb #2, Ramses IV: Colorful scenes from the Book of the Dead+graffiti! A blue ceiling. The goddess Nut. And a pink sarcophagus with writing and art to protect the mummy from danger!

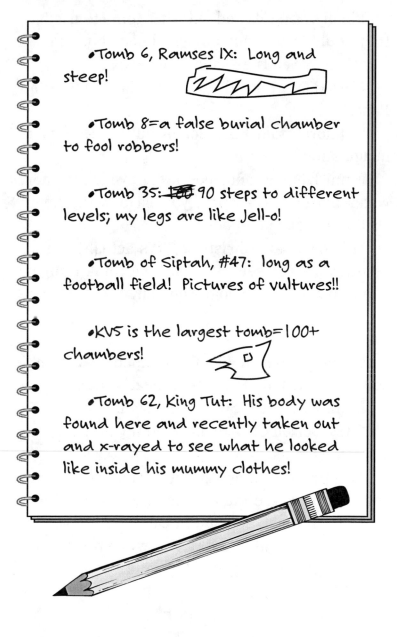

•Tomb 6, Ramses IX: Long and steep!

•Tomb 8=a false burial chamber to fool robbers!

•Tomb 35: ~~100~~ 90 steps to different levels; my legs are like Jell-o!

•Tomb of Siptah, #47: long as a football field! Pictures of vultures!!

•KV5 is the largest tomb=100+ chambers!

•Tomb 62, King Tut: His body was found here and recently taken out and x-rayed to see what he looked like inside his mummy clothes!

Finally, they'd had all the tomb-touristing they could handle and straggled back outside.

"Here, sit in the shade," said Papa.

Christina groaned. "There is NO shade, Papa."

"I know," said Papa sorrowfully. "Use your imagination."

Mimi laughed and took a big swig from her water bottle. "Christina, you have really been writing in your notebook."

"I know," said Christina. "It's actually fun to record what you see. It makes me think I might like to be an archaeologist one day."

"Why are you so grumpy, Grant?" Mimi asked.

Grant's little shoulders slumped. "I didn't see a scorpion all day. Just a measly mummy."

Mimi laughed. "Sorry," she said.

"Hey!" cried Christina. "I left my notebook in the tomb."

"Well run back and get it," Papa said. "We will head for the car. I don't think we'll be walking very fast, so you can catch up easily."

Christina nodded and ran off while the others began to slog through the hot sand.

Back inside the tomb, Christina looked all around in the darkness. Suddenly from a niche in the wall, an arm poked out. The gloved hand held her notebook.

"Give me the golden pyramid, and I will give you this," the voice said.

Christina was too scared to go into the dark niche. She thought the man was acting like a scorpion about to strike and she had no intention of becoming his prey.

She looked all around, but at that moment no one else was there. Most of the tourists had begun to head for shade and cool drinks and afternoon naps.

Suddenly, she had an idea. "Look!" she shouted. "A bat!"

As she had hoped, the hand dropped the notebook, which she reached down and grabbed. But as she ran off, she heard a very angry voice hiss at her, "Curses! I'll get you yet, young lady."

Water Over The Dam

That night, they slept on the *felucca*, ready to leave at first light. As Grant and Christina snuggled in their sleeping bags under the stars, Christina told her brother what had happened in the tomb that afternoon.

"Do you have a golden pyramid?" Grant asked.

"Not that I know of," said Christina with a yawn. "If I did, I would gladly give it back."

"Do the mummies scare you?" asked Grant.

"Not as much as the crocodiles and scorpions," Christina admitted. "But I sure wouldn't want to spend the night in the desert or in one of those tombs...I mean *brrr*...I'm cool here on the water. Aren't you, Grant?"

Silence.

"Grant?"

SGNOOOOOOOOOKKKK,   her   brother snored.

"Goodnight, Grant," Christina whispered. "Sweet dreams. Hope I have some, too, and not mummified nightmares!"

When the kids woke up the next morning, they were far down the river with the city of Aswan coming into view. Christina got the impression that perhaps they had set sail in the night. The adults were in the bow of the boat sipping chai tea and chatting merrily.

Christina crawled out of her sleeping bag and tucked herself under her grandmother's free arm just in time to hear her say, "Look at the Old Cataract Hotel there on the river bluff. That's where the famous English crime writer, Agatha Christie, wrote her best-selling novel, *Death on the Nile.*

"Death, death, death," a voice behind them grumbled. It was Grant in his King Tut pajamas.

He joined the group, yawning and rubbing his eyes. "Dead people, dead books, dead, dead, dead. Egypt would be a great place to spend Halloween. I wonder how you write trick-or-treat in **hieroglyphs**?"

When everyone ignored Grant's silly comments, he asked, "Knock-knock!"

When there was more silence (everyone knew about Grant's endless supply of silly jokes and riddles), Grant repeated, "KNOCK! KNOCK!"

Christina giggled. "We might as well answer. He'll just keep asking."

"Ok," said Papa. "I'll bite. Knock-knock who?"

"King Tut," Grant replied.

"King Tut who?" asked Papa.

"King Tut-key Fried Chicken!" said Grant with an uproarious laugh. He always thought his jokes were funnier than anyone else did. Everyone else groaned.

Suddenly, one of the crew came forward with his hand folded into a fist. He thrust out his arm. "Does this belong to anyone here?" he asked. He opened his palm to reveal a small, gold pyramid.

Christina gasped. "It's mine!" she blurted.

Mimi looked puzzled. "Where did you get that? I don't recall seeing it before."

"It...it..." Christina stammered. "It just might be a little souvenir..."

The man dropped the pyramid into her hand and headed back to the stern of the boat. "We'll be ashore in five minutes," he noted.

Mimi and Papa hopped up to get ready to go ashore. Grant stood with Christina on the bow to watch the boat sail into the harbor.

"Where did you really get that little gold pyramid, Christina?" Grant asked.

Christina shook her head, perplexed. "I don't know! Someone must have put it in my pocket or backpack when I wasn't looking." She opened her hand and stared at the small, golden charm. "It looks harmless," she said. "So why is someone chasing me to get it...and threatening me if they don't?"

"I don't know," said Grant, "but you'd better hold on."

"Why?" Christina asked in alarm, looking all around.

Grant laughed. "Because, silly...we're coming ashore."

Just then, the boat bumped into the dock at Aswan.

They spent the rest of the day looking over the town of Aswan, visiting the Nubian Museum, the Sharia as-Souk, and Elephantine Island. They learned that the enormous Aswan Dam had been built to regulate the flow of the Nile River and that Lake Nasser is the largest man-made lake in the world.

"Boy, sightseeing in Egypt is exhausting," Mimi said at lunch. "There is just too much to see."

"I liked the Nilometer," said Grant. "I thought Papa was making that name up, but it really is a neat idea to measure the depth of the river by building steps of a certain length down into the river."

"Those Egyptians thought of everything," Papa agreed. "And I don't know the Arabic word for *siesta*, but I sure need one."

Mimi decided to shop. Papa went back to the felucca to take a nap. And Grant and Christina promised to go directly to the boat as soon as they had finished their dessert.

"We'll all meet back there in one hour," Mimi ordered.

But one hour later, Mimi was still shopping, Papa was still sleeping, and Grant and Christina were invited to Mummyland!

The Spitting Camel

It all started when Grant and Christina were sitting innocently at the table trying to invent a game called Old, Middle, and New Kingdom. With pencils and napkins, they drew a game board. Christina pulled out the little gold pyramid to use as a playing piece. Grant found a small, round, smooth stone on the ground.

To their shock and surprise, a man in a palanquin stopped right in front of them. He stared at them with great curiosity. Then, he surprised them by hopping down from his carrying chair and grabbing the golden pyramid right off the table.

"No!" screeched Christina. "That's mine!"

"No longer," the man hissed, and in spite of being dressed in a king-size bed's worth of sheet-looking fabric, complete with turban, he jumped back on his chair and was hauled off faster than they could have ever expected.

"Let's go!" Grant cried. "We can catch him." Grant grabbed some cheese and crackers he had not finished and stuffed them in his shorts pocket.

Christina jumped up and they ran down the mazelike alleys of the souk running as fast as they could. Ahead, they saw the man jump off the chair and begin to run. Shockingly, he began to undress, leaving white fabric trailing behind him like a mummy.

"Look!" Christina shouted. "He has on khaki clothes underneath...our mad archaeologist!"

The faster the kids ran, the faster the man ran. They could see that he clutched the gold pyramid in his clenched fist. The other hand waved people and carts and camels out of his way.

"Ooh, camel spit!" Christina complained, as they passed too closely to an upset beast. She wiped her wet arm on her tee shirt.

"Come on," urged Grant, "he's going down

that alley. I think we can catch him."

When they turned into the alley, it was dark and spooky. The little street was so narrow that little sunlight seeped down into it. Grant and Christina moved more slowly, looking left and right to try to spot the man.

Just then, they heard the creak of a door and then a SLAM. "He went in there!" said Grant.

Quickly they dashed to the doorway. A sign read:

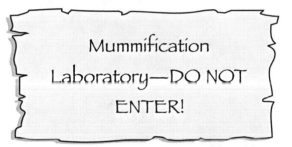

Mummification Laboratory—DO NOT ENTER!

Grant looked at Christina. Christina looked at Grant. They both shrugged their shoulders, took a deep breath...and went inside!

Are You My Mummy?

It was dark inside the building. The air was stale and dusty. There were no lights on. From the tables and tools and charts on the wall, Christina could tell that this was a laboratory. Strangely, everything was in disarray. Papers and tools were scattered around. Cobwebs hung from the corners and shuttered windows. There was a musty smell.

"Do I smell mummies?" Grant whispered.

"I don't see any mummies, thank goodness," Christina whispered back. "Let's just look for my pyramid and get out of here as fast as we can."

Slowly, and with great hesitation and some fear, they tiptoed into the next room. It was even darker. The light was so dim that they had to hold onto the edges of the lab tables to make their way around the room. Christina shivered, just hoping she wouldn't accidentally touch any wrapped—or worse yet, unwrapped!—mummy.

"Look!" Grant whispered. He pointed into the next room. On the edge of a table in a slat of light coming through a broken shutter sat an object. It glinted the color of gold, like a lost pirate treasure coin beneath the sea.

"Good job!" whispered Christina back. "The pyramid...let's grab it and run for dear life!"

Still on tiptoes, they moved quickly into the room. Christina reached out and put her hand over the pyramid. Just then, much to her horror, a dark-gloved hand reached out from a closet door and clamped over her hand.

Christina screamed!

Oh, Rats!

Grant screamed! Christina screamed again. The rest of the man slithered out of the closet. Both kids were petrified, but in some ways relieved to see that at least it was a real man...and not a mummy.

"Not so fast, young lady!" the man snarled. "It took me long enough to find this golden pyramid...and I have no intention of you taking it."

"But I don't understand," Christina said. "What is this all about? It just looks like a dumb souvenir. Besides, I didn't take it, it just appeared on our felucca."

"I find that hard to believe," said the man, his hand still clamped hard over hers. He did not pay any attention (and perhaps did not even see)

Grant cowering in the corner. "You were at the airport when my son stole the plans of tomb 7B...the one that is said to still be filled with treasure. The one we plan to plunder! But we needed the little gold pyramid...it has a secret code inside that allows entrance into the tomb."

"You're a tomb-robber?" Christina asked with a gasp.

"Of course!" said the man. "What did you think? This lab is just an old unused one that we use for cover as serious archaeologists." He removed his hand and Christina pulled her hand away quickly but stood perfectly still.

The man twisted the top of the pyramid which fell off onto the table. When he tapped the pyramid on the table, a tiny computer chip fell out. "Aha! Just what I expected."

"But why would you tell me all this?" Christina asked.

The man let out an evil laugh. "Because I don't plan for you to be around to tell anyone else. Don't you recall the curse that I said would befall you if you tried to elude me?"

Out of the corner of her eye, Christina could see Grant doing the oddest thing. He was crumbling the leftover cheese and crackers he had brought from the restaurant into a pile on the floor. This made no sense to her whatsoever and all she could think was that her brother was very nervous.

But then one of the shuttered cabinet doors creaked...and out slipped a mouse. Then another. Then another. They ran for the cheese, then as if giddy with delight, ran away from the pile to eat. Suddenly, Grant stamped his foot and the mice raced around the room. One jumped up onto the table!

Christina did not like mice, but the man, apparently, was absolutely petrified of them. He dropped the pyramid, began to scream and backed away into the closet he had come out of, holding his hands over his face.

Fast as lightning, Christina grabbed the pyramid. "Run, Grant!" she cried, heading out the door of the room.

Grant turned to follow her, but stopped long enough to yell at the man in the closet. "Hey, buddy, that's called the Rat Curse—glad you liked it!" Then he ran to follow his sister out of the room and out of the mummification laboratory.

A Date in the Oasis

"Run!" Christina screamed as the door to the lab slammed behind them.

Christina and her brother ran back down the alley, turning once to see that the man had recovered, and clothing flying, was chasing after them with two Evil Eyes staring at them.

At the end of the alley, the two children hesitated, not remembering if they should turn left or right into the souk. It did not matter. For when they began to run again, they immediately bumped smack into Papa and an Egyptian policeman.

"Papa!" Christina screamed. "A man is following us!"

Just then the man rounded the corner. The policeman nabbed him.

"I know," said Papa. "But not anymore."

Christina was very confused. The policeman carted the man off to jail. Papa grabbed Christina and Grant tightly by their arms and tugged them through the crowded souk. Christina was relieved, but she was very afraid that her grandfather was angry.

Papa did not speak until he rounded a corner and they came to a very pretty oasis-looking café. There sat an anxious Mimi waiting for them. Beside her stood another Egyptian policeman with the young man they had seen in the airport in handcuffs.

"Christina! Grant!!" Mimi cried. She rose and grabbed them from Papa and smothered them with hugs and kisses.

"We're ok," Grant promised. "Turn loose!"

"Oh, Mimi," said Christina, "I'm sorry we got so involved in a mystery without telling you."

"You know better, young lady," said Papa, pretending to be angry but she and Grant could tell he was very relieved not to have two mummified grandchildren.

"What's all this about?" Christina asked. "I still don't have a clue!"

Mimi laughed. "Sit down and have some lemonade and I will tell you," she said.

And so, out came an elaborate story that the man in the airport who had stolen the plans was the son of the mad archaeologist in the laboratory. They were both indeed tomb-robbers, but very inept, which is why the police knew what they were up to...they just couldn't find them.

"They always robbed graves that had already been looted a long time ago," Mimi explained. "That's how sorry they were at their job. But this time it was serious. This newly-discovered tomb is filled with treasure, but everyone felt it was secure because of a high-tech digital code that was the only way to access it."

"But someone stole the code," Papa continued the story.

"And put it in the little gold pyramid?" guessed Christina.

"Right," said Mimi, "which the man at the airport dropped into your backpack so that the police would not get it...even if they captured him."

"So they were chasing me all this time to get something I didn't even know I had?" said Christina.

"No one knew, until it appeared on the felucca," said Mimi. "Even then we did not know the meaning of your 'cheap little souvenir' until I had a call from Mr. Hawass telling me about this important find and what was going on."

"You know Mimi," Papa bragged. "She put two and two together and came up with four reasons why I should track you kids down when you didn't show up when you should have!"

"But how did you know where to look for us?" asked Grant. "We were basically lost!"

The policeman spoke up. "The souk has a thousand eyes!" he said. "It is not likely that two American children and a mad-looking archaeologist on a chase through the souk would go unnoticed."

"We just asked," said Papa, "and followed the pointing fingers like following breadcrumbs in the forest."

"Hey," said Christina, "speaking of breadcrumbs, what were all those cheese and cracker crumbs about, Grant?"

Grant laughed proudly. "Remember—I am the Amazing Karnak! I saw a little mouse and thought I could create a distraction to get us out of there. Sort of like making a rabbit pop out of a hat, I made the mice hop out of the cupboards. Of course I couldn't know that the man was so afraid of them. I thought it would be you who would scream and run."

The man in handcuffs spoke up. "My father is petrified of mice," he said. "He calls them the curse of the earth. He was once trapped in a tomb with a rat and..."

"Mice?!" Mimi interrupted. "Rats?! I don't understand, and I don't think I want to understand. But I do think it's time to go home."

The policeman nodded and hauled the handcuffed man to the police car.

"Aw, King Tut in a tu-tu," said Grant. "We were just starting to have fun."

Mimi scowled. "Next time, I'm taking you kids to Russia or someplace, where you can't get into any trouble."

"The Mystery on the Orient Express," Christina whispered to her brother.

"I heard that!" said Mimi with a grin, rising.

"Follow me or I'm going to wrap you like a mummy with one tail-end free for me to hold like a leash to keep up with you two."

They all headed for the carriage, Grant lagging behind. "Hey, does anyone want to know what King Tut says when asked his nickname?"

Mimi, Papa, and Christina turned and said one word:

"NO!!!!!!!!!!!!!!!!!!!"

The End

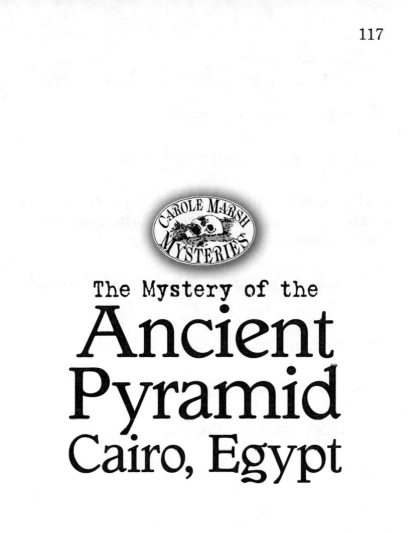

The Mystery of the

Ancient
Pyramid
Cairo, Egypt

Glossary

amulet: good-luck charm

Arabic: language spoken in Egypt

archaeologist: person educated and trained to locate, research, and explain historic ruins and their contents

archaeology: the study of ancient ruins and artifacts

bazaar: outdoor shopping area

bedouin: nomadic desert people

begah: woman's head scarf

caleche: carriage

cartouche: group of **hieroglyphs**; personal symbol

Corniche: main road in Luxor

dynasty: a period of time a certain group of rulers were in power

fellaheen: Egyptian farmer

galabiyya: long smock

hieroglyph: symbol that means a letter, sound, or word

kohl: thick black paint; often used as eye makeup

mosque: Muslim place of worship

mummification: process of preserving a dead body

mummy: human or animal that has been embalmed, preserved, and wrapped in cloths

oasis: area of water, plants and trees in the midst of a desert

obelisk: four-sided tapered tower with a pyramid-shaped top

papyrus: paper made from the stem of a plant

palanquin: a chair carried by bearers

Built-In Book Club!

Talk About It!

Questions for Discussion:

1. Does Egypt seem like an exotic country to visit? If you live there, what country seems "exotic" to you?

2. Why does Christina get so interested in **archaeology**? What things lead us to be interested in certain careers?

3. Would you like to travel around the world with interesting grandparents and help solve mysteries?

4. What parts of this story do you think the author made up, and what parts are actually factual?

5. Why do you think Christina is so headstrong and determined to solve the mystery without any help from adults? Do you think she is brave...or foolish?

6. Why did the author let Grant tell funny King Tut riddles?

7. Did you think Grant was clever to get the mice to come out and scare the mad archaeologist?

8. What did you learn about Egypt that you did not know before?

9. If you have read other Carole Marsh Mysteries, what did you learn about Grant and Christina that you did not know before?

10. If you wrote your own "real kids/real places" mystery, what real place locale would you choose for the setting?

Built-In Book Club!
◢Bring It To Life!◥

1. Make pyramids! Use your geometry tools and skills to cut squares and triangles and build some pyramids. These could be tabletop individual pyramids made from index card stock, or larger pyramids for the floor built out of heavier cardboard. Decorate the outside of the pyramids.

2. Using the **Hieroglyph** Alphabet provided, have each student write their name in **hieroglyphs**. You can draw these on card stock, color, cut out, and string on black cord to wear around the neck.

3. Make a pyramid cake by baking a sheet-style poundcake, cutting out a square and triangle and "gluing" together with frosting. Then frost the entire outside of the cake with a light cocoa frosting or white frosting tinted with food color. You can add a green frosting oasis and blue frosting lake around your pyramid if you wish.

4. Play Egyptian or Arabic-style music and have students get some aerobic activity by belly-dancing, whirling like a dervish, or walking like an Egyptian.

5. Draw a King Tut style headdress and cut out the center "face" so that students can put their face in and have their pictures made!

6. Have students make up and tell their own King Tut or other Egyptian-based riddles.

7. Host a "Thousand and One Nights" storytelling session. Let students write and illustrate a story based in Egypt, then take turns telling their stories aloud, one per day.

Hieroglyph Alphabet

Note: Each **hieroglyph** appears above its letter.

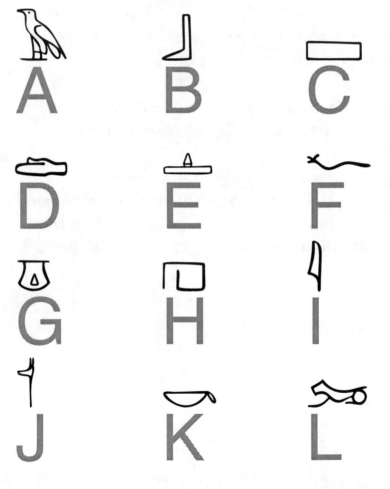

A B C

D E F

G H I

J K L

ANCIENT
Egyptian Fast Facts

 Wow, Ramses II had 100 children!

 An ideogram is a sign that stands for an idea!
A phonogram is a sign that stands for a sound!
So, a **hieroglyph** is a combination of ideograms and phonograms!

 A lot of gold came from the Nubian mines!

 "Black Land" = the Nile Valley
"Red Land" = the desert

 Even sandals were made from papyrus!

 In ancient markets, baboons were used to "sniff out" shoplifters!

 Cinderella was an old Egyptian tale!

Ancient Egyptian makeup!
• Kohl = black eye paint made from minerals
• Skin moisturizer = made from cat, crocodile, and hippo fat!

It's so hot in Egypt that Egyptians once wore cones of fat on their heads to melt and keep them cool during dinner!

Egyptian boys had shaved heads except for a long "sidelock" on one side!

Magical charms were worn on necklaces to prevent sickness.

Egyptian nobles often took their wives and children with them when they went hunting.

Cats were considered sacred and wore gold rings!

The huge pyramid of Pharaoh Khufu took more than twenty years to build.

Honey was widely used as a sweetener in Egypt and many farms had beehives.

 Tutankhamen, the "boy King," took the throne at age ten.

 Boats made from papyrus were the main form of transportation.

 Leapfrog and tug-of-war were popular games in Egypt.

 In some cases, cats, dogs, and crocodiles were mummified. They even got their own coffins!

About the Author

Carole Marsh is an author and publisher who has written many works of fiction and non-fiction for young readers. She travels throughout the United States and around the world to research her books. In 1979 Carole Marsh was named Communicator of the Year for her corporate communications work with major national and international corporations.

Marsh is the founder and CEO of Gallopade International, established in 1979. Today, Gallopade International is widely recognized as a leading source of educational materials for every state and many countries. Marsh and Gallopade were recipients of the 2004 Teachers' Choice Award. Marsh has written more than 50 Carole Marsh Mysteries™. In 2007, she was named Georgia Author of the Year. Years ago, her children, Michele and Michael, were the original characters in her mystery books. Today, they continue the Carole Marsh Books tradition by working at Gallopade. By adding grandchildren Grant and Christina as new mystery characters, she has continued the tradition for a third generation.

Ms. Marsh welcomes correspondence from her readers. You can e-mail her at fanclub@gallopade.com, visit carolemarshmysteries.com, or write to her in care of Gallopade International, P.O. Box 2779, Peachtree City, Georgia, 30269 USA.

Write your own Mystery!

M ake up a dramatic title!

Y ou can pick four real kid characters!

S elect a real place for the story's setting!

T ry writing your first draft!

E dit your first draft!

R ead your final draft aloud!

Y ou can add art, photos or illustrations!

Share your book with others and
send me a copy!

Would you like to be a character in a Carole Marsh Mystery?

If you would like to star in a Carole Marsh Mystery, fill out the form below and write a 25-word paragraph about why you think you would make a good character! Once you're done, ask your mom or dad to send this page to:

Carole Marsh Mysteries Fan Club
Gallopade International
P.O. Box 2779
Peachtree City, GA 30269

My name is:

I am a:_____boy _____ girl   Age:_____

I live at: _____

City:_____ State:_____ Zip code:_____

My e-mail address: _____

My phone number is: _____

_____

_____

_____

_____

_____

_____

_____

_____

Visit the <u>carolemarshmysteries.com</u> website to:

· Join the Carole Marsh Mysteries™ Fan Club!

· Write a letter to Christina, Grant, Mimi, or Papa!

· Cast your vote for where the next mystery should take place!

· Find fascinating facts about the countries where the mysteries take place!

· Track your reading on an international map!

· Take the Fact or Fiction online quiz!

· Play the Around-the-World Scavenger Hunt computer game!

· Find out where the *Mystery Girl* is flying next!